We can often get so caught in the everyday that it is easy to forget the fragments between...

A Different Language

If for only a fleeting moment a trace of past would pass.
If games and planes would be the way they were.
A simple parallel.
To look at crossing tides and kiss the sand they swell,
And thank for what they bring.

For we know to lament can be to not look forward,
To not create new memories to later cherish.
Hold dear what once was,
And as light from day suddenly dims,
To smile a new tomorrow.
We must look on,
Must welcome what new dawn sings.

If we never, then we will never have had.
If we close our eyes to gain old warmth,
Opportunities will flash on by,
And never shall return.
If not phrased in different ways,
You'll never know a brighter day.

When sense is drawn from chaos,
And simple plans are made.
When lovers swear by broken dreams,
We will,
Always were,
And truly,
Always will be.

Another

Through a tiny gap I watched you,
Though I felt your eyes on me,
As if you were performing and tortured me with glee.

Each day and night this play we'd act,
Though never set the same,
Soon enough it came to be our secret little game.

But then one night I saw him,
By the corner of your bed,
He came in through the mirror and not one word was said.

In a moment I then realised,
Our two became a three,
And not one day before his presence could I longer see.

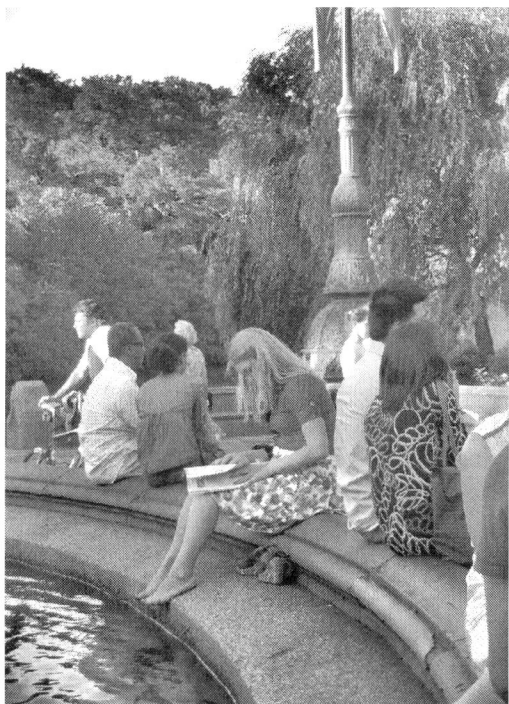

Rock of Sand

If only dreams were another world,
A time, a breath away.
If only stories could creak to life,
And explode from pen to felt.

If every step was worth a stride,
A thousand times the length.
If only words could paint with oils,
And never dare to dry.

But to break these laws would be to cheat,
To venture from the truth.
For one can find a dream explode,
Yet always be unique.

Without these trials, without these aches,
A never will but be.
Without these blisters this bitter sweet would taste no memory.

A spark won't always erupt to flames,
Expecting is a curse.
A leap may never get you far,
Yet frees you from the dirt.

So carry on, walk on my friend,
And cast your spell unique.
We can, we will, we labour on,
Just cherish whilst you seek.

But ours

You tell me how to feel,
A many a splendid thing.
Do not these words speak truths?
If they do not then at least they speak of something,
Make you debate, question and hesitate.

For poetry is not a divide of intellects,
Not a way to quote from dusty shelves.
It is not a simple sentence wrapped in snobbery,
Not a pointless enigma for intellectuals.

Every action ever made,
Each song ever sung,
Every lover, murderer, preacher.
It hums like electricity.

Only the connection of thought to paper,
From ungraspable to inanimate,
Creates these flows.

But rather than ending,
Once written, spoke or mimed,
Its journey has just begun.

To one her line of joy,
To another his endless pain,
Beauty.
Fluidity.

For what these eyes have pierced,
What ears have caught in swells,
These fingers etched on lines,
Is not my secret,
But our collective thirst.

Every poet is you,
Is us,
But ours.

Cable and Vines

When chalk board moves are waning,
When computers hum no sound,
When business cards are numbers,
Then instinct is found.

And though we like our bicycles,
Our cogs, our screens, our nouns,
There is no stronger meaning,
When the wolves our flesh have found.

To every perfect beauty,
With eyes across the way,
This glance can climax meeting,
That smile can make a day.

A mystery now is the mind,
A complexity of dense,
For no matter how it 'should' be happy
It's not as simple as sense.

No social structure standing,
No ticking every box,
Can guarantee the clouds won't cover,
Or open all the locks.

We are a complex creature,
We are though not alone.
And everyone is different,
A comfort to be known.

Deliver

It was an undefinable love.
One of anger, beauty, rage and lust.
No different to any other,
But the most special of all.

Such eyes to pierce souls,
Soft hair to move this earth.
Scorched ever more, forever more,
And untimely in deliverance.

A meeting of footsteps,
A lie with only truth.
These ways are unobtainable,
But worth the fight they hold.

No currency can pay,
No hours worked will source,
But double what you earn,
By walking round your heart.

Feel at Home

You belong with fantastical creatures,
To bathe beneath the sun,
For a fairy tale you have flown from,
And I can only run.

So sit tight now on desires,
Bask for longer in these rays,
For it is a new land that I'm creating,
It's a land to match your ways.

From Oaks to Ember

Don't digress.
Never falter less.
For our time is short.
Ordained by some strange spirit.
Faltering forever more,
In a whirlwind of complexities.

Our being captured here,
In an unknown gear.
Always changing,
Upon a waning.
We are our own.
To be alone.

Sent from where to never know,
To sometimes grow,
Then dwindle,
Like kindle.
From oaks to ember,
But bless our sender.

Hold firm dear friend.
Stand your ground.
Each leaf will fall.
On our knees we crawl.
But do not forget us,
For we are yours.

We are that distant call.

Her Disregarded Essence

Under locks you kept a pillow,
Of soft and woven wool,
And while every night you rested,
A single hair the weave would pull.

Though now you have departed,
And beside me do not lay,
I continue to keep the pillow,
So your memory will not fray.

Still each night I rest beside it,
But do not rest my head,
Then forever here I'll keep your presence,
With pillow hair and bed.

Hitler's Garden

If Hitler had a garden would there be some weeds,
And would the weeds that he removed be weeds to you and me.
And if I went to feed them would I know the mix,
Could I ever understand each flower has its pick?

Could I mange simply to deeply suit their needs,
Some dark, some tough, some rocky,
Some only just now seeds.

Or perhaps he wouldn't bother with various organisms.
Maybe he would choose just one to sit there in its prison.
Each time I now picture his little plot of land,
It's pretty, ugly, pale and vibrant and nurtured with his hands.

What would the roses smell like?
Could I smell them if I went,
Or would he sternly send me off,
When over them I leant.

As Hitler sorted people,
We too have raked our sand,
But though it's tried with gardens,
It can never work with Man.

Just keep an eye and listen,
Just listen to its needs,
Perhaps a garden best kept now,
Is one that's left to breathe.

I'll See You in an Experience

Tonight I embark on another foot driven journey,
Through buildings and parks to absorb the night's delights.
Enlightened by inhalation I look over the setting.

Tonight I watch a man play with fire;
Watch him swing orbs of flames in a circular motion,
Though my mind cannot help but speak of the dangers,
And scream at the rules I should know.

I cannot help but be still.
As I, like my fellow onlookers watch with admiration,
At the beauty before us.
Whilst they snap memories of the occasion.

I can only feel warm from the sight and the intriguing motions.
Tonight it was not the call of the songbird that captured me,
Nor the smile on a child's face as they beheld an image of love,
In those work worn eyes of parents.
Nor were it the smell of the evening's crisp cool air,
Announcing the coming of another harsh winter.

Instead it was danger and the excitement of watching,
Watching my man with flames,
Watching him glide golden spheres through the gripping air,
Whilst the parents took their children home,
And the birds called yet another sweet song.

Jumping Walls

If I had half the mind I would write you a letter,
Fold it into a shape and glide it straight to you.
But with these lights between a flashing chorus,
An overture has sounded.

Deep breathes, exhales and memories pounded.
I am yours like these words I write.
They were once wet, now set,
But yours none the same.
Take them, disregard them, it is your choice.
I am swollen with tears at the thought that you might read them.

But these words they cannot reach you,
At least not by my own hands.
I know we mourn loss as we feel alone,
Angry at the barrier that we don't even know exists.
It is only you the departed who know,
Know if they have left us for more or nothing,
It is a one-way screen and all I see is sky.

My comfort is that I too one day may know,
And be wherever it is you are,
But this is also my greatest fear.
You said you would go on ahead and put in a good word for me,
I would prefer it if you came back and took my words out.

Motion Picture

Play on, I'll sit here whilst you do.
No moment wasted,
My time is my time,
And I'll keep it how I like it.

This place is my activity,
Just to be here is enough,
No games,
No shouting,
No speech.

The sky is a spilt paint pot,
Of assorted colours and tones,
And in a desperate attempt to halt the stains,
Someone is blotching franticly,
To stop it before it dries.
Though in the process swirling whites remain.

They are these clouds,
They are now part of this sky,
And they change how they wish,
Though I choose to remain.
I just hope in all the panic,
The Skymaker has stopped to notice.

When fine lines and graphs are not enough,
When calculations get you down,
Rely on the unpredictable and the random.
There is comfort in knowing that some things are beyond control.
Not all labs can explain with drops of formaldehyde,
Not all pictures need an ending,
For mine is an infinity.

Naked spaces

Sit low, and with gentle thoughts in smiles,
That harness only tears we float.
In empty rooms that once told of people,
Walking, talking and sharing moments.

Yet they are gone now.
Though every so often you forget,
To only be reminded again by the curse of mortality.
These faces you will see no more,
Other than in faded photographs and cherished memories.

They flash in and out.
Places that once held their souls remain,
But only their ghosts walk these halls.

Yet they do not and will never be again.
Like a painful curse upon your being,
A reminder is both a kiss upon the cheek and a jab,
Deep within the heart.

The years forever seemed they would return,
We became complacent in expecting,
An ever long and everlasting tale.
Appreciate every moment.
Each existing sadness is a story.
Hard times you will come to learn from,
So now is future comfort.

Yet new days have come to fall.
Clocks will shed the seconds,
The hand that fixed its hours will not no more,
Nor rest its arm upon the mantle.

Memories are greater than photographs,
For in memories things can change.
And we remember the good,
As time will heal all wounds.
I just wish it would leave more scars.

For to breathe is to lament,
To fix eyes hard within that scene,
Of wonderful and dear moments that never shall return.
Dear friends and kin you will not be forgotten.
I shall remain for now.
Tell sweet tales of old we shared,
Raise a glass of your liquor and laugh at what we knew.
Together we were stronger,
But here alone you give me strength.

And in this very moment I fear I stare at ghosts.
Future paths we can be changing,
Though the ending rigid waits.
I would here swear to rather be with ghosts that came from flesh,
Than to endlessly and chaotically dare share an empty space.

Hold fast I ask now simply,
In shadows now I walk.
I tread these halls of memories,
And speak of how we talked.

Ornamental Scars

As here we sit, while here we ponder,
Observe the sky, watch a while longer.
Like wisped foam they will pass,
With longer life so too this grass.

Walk with me, become enlightened by senses,
These dwelling creatures are by no means you're lesser.
It is a place for withdrawal, for releasing,
We grow old,
Remains pleasing.

I will cut open this fresh pair, steal its nectar,
By all means join in, by none a spectator.
Clasp the leaves in your hand; allow your fingers to fan,
See them flutter, spiral, shudder, allow them to land.

Waste not a moment in this place, prioritize not replace,
For in my garden we discuss not dictate.

Reflections

And as we draw this uncertain light from every corner,
As we collect each ray from every mourner,
Whilst day still holds another view,
We ask ourselves what you would do.

With no more time to grasp at hate,
The darkness falls, forgiveness waits.
And now that air is full of bare,
At what, we think now do we stare.

For let it be known that whilst we search,
Life still grows from dark scorched earth.
Now ever know, now never fear,
That light you saved is forever here.

Skywards

If I, amid all these unstoppable stars could dream,
And never awake but to see your eyes above me.
I would mistake them for an image within the universe,
And return to meet my visions.

If you could see my face,
You then would see my faults,
Would you never kiss my ear,
Or whisper dreams of fate.

If we, but only for a second,
Could recognise significant moments,
Then we could cherish and change,
And never be without.

Soapbox Doormat
My friends!
In the eyes of the power we should live by lines of serenity.
Where minority is the expense,
And pleasure the apple decayed.

IGNORE PROPAGANDA OR YOU WILL BE INFECTED!

Fellow men!
A walk is no longer a walk,
Rather a constant conquering,
Never to be a free land,
Rather a hand rubbing ecstasy.

**SAY NO TO PROPAGANDA OR IT WILL CLIMB THROUGH YOUR
WINDOWS AND WHISPER CONTEMPT!**

Special guests!
The propaganda jaw spreads the propaganda disease,
Force-feeding children propaganda tape worms.
They chew on the flesh of self-discovery,
And grind on the bones of reason.
Propaganda,
Propaganda,
Propaganda.

**FLEE NOW BRETHRENS. ITS WHEELS SPLICE CRUNCH AND
SPLATTER!**

Beloved generation!
Listen to me for I am the voice of reason,
The voice of reason,
The voice of reason.
Listen to me

LISTEN TO ME!

Sparrow Hit the Window

During the night my visions were of mirrors,
Three hundred and sixty,
Though I don't remember counting.
Each announced me,
Each grew tired of my image,
And my image alone.

Uneasy and unfiltered all of this was,
I only waited or company,
Nothing more,
For there was nothing else to do.
Of my own image I was sick,
Though I stood,
Eyes solidly fixed.

The fix became a vision within a vision,
I saw poets, travellers and musicians.
All stuttered and spoke,
Called aloud in a crowd of competing voices,
I heard not a word,
Only a mad desperate chorus.

Back in my room I turned to meet myself once more.
This was to be my last look,
My last chance to link name, face and life.
Gently I left the room through a back door in a mirror.
I had been comforted by thoughts of eternal rest and slumber,
Yet haunted by flashes and the ever-creeping fear.
A fear of being forgotten.

Split Screens

What man given the opportunity to live it again would not?
For then he could live it twice.
In parallel.
And view himself from the other side.

It is that newness.
It will always seem that fresh.
For no matter how old the man,
He is always new to life.

And in age he expects wisdom.
Looks skywards in expectation.
Unaware.
As years can only be a carrier.
And not simply the rule.

Yet the romantic strums.
Plays his mandolin from sheet.
And sings divine that regardless,
He would have it no other way.

Perhaps this is the way.
To live it again would be to lie.
Perhaps to play an unknown note.
But I dare not turn the sand.

For only the fear of losing a touch,
For anger at not grasping tighter.
And now I see me forever.
Reflected in those eyes.

Those beautiful eyes.

The Fragments Between

To never know these arms I hold are yours,
To realise their worth some years from now.
When their empty ghost is all I own,
Upon the path of perfect bliss you lay.

But you lay too soon before the end.
Too soon to see that path was like the world,
And came back around.
For you I had found.

And for you I had come back around.
Without knowing,
But you had left the ground.
On empty streets this curse remained,
Never again and forever pained.

An endless loop was always made,
Always cursed,
Always paved.
You came too soon and you I lost.

To never again come back around,
Forever knowing you had left the ground.
Eyes too deeply set upon the horizon.
And never there,
Never to appreciate.

It is darkness now.
How I hope you're happy now.

I wore my green eyes this morning.
For I know they were your favourite.

The Nature of Serenity

With the first sweet breath and dawn of innocence,
Two lives, two tales are born untwined.
To believe it fate that both these souls should meet,
May be considered inconceivable,
Too holy and far too wishful.

Like random pebbles scattered upon tide worn beaches,
For what dictates to whom each meets,
We leave for you to ponder,
To search and to believe.
But these bonds are made.
And in time such lovers saved,
As sometimes no explanation is the best answer we will ever find.

To know is to never understand our own,
And each other's deepest complexities.
Without the darkest hour the joyful moments we hold so dear,
Would never taste as sweet,
And triumph would be but a daily untruth.
If the sun should never set upon an argument,
It then in turn should never rise upon regret.

Two sets of eyes see first the light,
Four hands unclasped hold more.
To eat, to share, to breathe,
To sing with heads held high,
Amid even the hardest rain,
Is to love.
Each hardship is yet another memory and a bond to further bind.
Bless this holy union divine forever more.
Dream of further like this and then quite simply,
Adore.

The Watcher

Both looked up at the dominant clock.
Its cold glare announced the passing of another second.
Then another.
And another.

Each strike to the next seemed to mock its onlooker.
A second,
Each seemed to be pondering,
Was a very long time.

They looked at each other.
Each glared with disgust at one another,
But neither spoke a word.

He lit a cigarette,
His companion did the same.
He inhaled.
So did the other.
Just like the clock,
He felt his watcher,
Mocking him.

Now and then he would search the room with his dreary
dead eyes.
He noticed that whenever he would turn to face the guest that he
would be staring right back,
Watching his every move,
Breath,
And stare.

I would often look at him and think him paranoid through his
actions.
He would quickly turn when his visitor was least expecting it,

Yet no,
He was always ready,
Ready and grinning,
Grinning right back.

He looked to be contemplating moving from his spot,
But he seemed to fear the man would leave him.
No matter how heartless and cruel he appeared in his muted ways,
He was still someone to share the moment with to him,
And was pleasing to the eye too.

Sometimes he would turn to me,
Staring at me.
Just as he had learnt from his now perfect friend,
He would glare at me.

I was once his idol,
Every waking moment devoted to my care and being,
But he had a new love now.

Past their first meeting,
A time of new awareness and self-discovery with apprehension and fear,
They were becoming closer,
And closer.

You may think me jealous,
Or some may find it cruel and heartless for him to show love for another,
But it did not vex me so.
For I knew one thing of his companion,
Which he did not.

I was not afraid of the threat posed in years of seven,

So I did it.

With a soft swift tap I took a hammer to his companion's face,
Then watched the matter fall,
Watched his love die and break away,
Then I smiled.

With a quick and hurried rush,
He left the room.

With my now victorious stance I looked at the destruction on the
floor below me,
And there,
Before me,
I saw the most wondrous of things.

There were hundreds and hundreds of beautiful people staring
back at me,
Just as content with my attack.
So I stood a while,
Then a while longer,
As the clock struck more seconds,
And admired the beauty before me.

These Unstoppable Stars.

Amid all these unstoppable stars,
Lies a single fact of fiction.
They are forever clear,
But only as our eyes allow.

Then destiny from here is chaos,
the future clear to dust,
And unfathomable truths,
Laid bare and deeply uncertain.

We cannot shift these stars,
But we can choose if they shine above us,
Or if we hide beneath this soil.
Dare we stare at worms?
For we are the earth scratchers.

Can shadows whisper what forms have seen,
Of past and present and future scenes?
Can air breath itself in,
And exhale the lungs it drew.

Without poetry we are nothing.
It is the personification of being.
It is the essence of philosophy,
A million stories in a single sentence.

These stars above are our poems,
A combination of our choice,
For an infinite outcome,
For that endless sentence.

Then as we look up toward this bitter night sky,
As we ride on through the haze,
We see that distant path to nowhere,
But a path nonetheless.

To Draw Horizons

To never have held the hand of sin,
No vice, no malice, no evil win.

If never sold a feral lie,
Then would you believe to never try.

For in this world, this grand old harp,
We strum these strings, these strings of sharp.

Today is fresh, today is new.
Grab this breath and this chance you threw.

So when it's asked of what you've made,
You'll say you learnt, you knew, you saved.

If heaven and earth began one way,
Of what this dawn would nature say.

Variance.

If once that was had never been.
If time and tides could hold like evergreen.
If fire in flickers could keep a hand,
And cold that snaps would freeze the sand.

Then nothing then could be more calm,
Nothing then would speak of harm.
But roses rot and teeth will break,
Creaking stops and joints can ache.

The comfort comes in that we change,
Forever now is now in range.
Embrace. Enrage.
Fear not next page.

We are the never men,
We can but grow.
We are the what,
But when, who knows.

Wake Sleep Repeat

Spread these wings of crimson red,
Behold my image through dreams of dread.

This white glow is blinding,
Forever my surrounding.
Binding,
So tiring.

My silver frame absorbs the white light.
It is my friend,
Companion,
Protector.

Do not anger me,
I forgive no man, pardon nor plead.
My crime was faith,
Punishment eternity.

Do not forget me,
I can shout no louder in this space,
No cry has pierced its thick skin to the ears of a soul,
Nor returned a hope of liberty.

Within these lines I shall stay,
So for longer I shall bask.
Stretch my wings in these glorious rays,
For in these beautiful lines of creation I am at peace,
And for a moment,
I forget.

Weak Feet, Shiny Walls

Walk on my friend,
Through cascading halls of hush.
All onlookers wear your uniform,
If not, they will be fitted soon.

They watch each newcomer,
Watch your hobbles,
Coughs and needs.

There is no survival of the fittest here,
Only private bets on who will be the first,
And last to fall.

Sleep well long corridor,
For no one else will.
Except the latecomers.

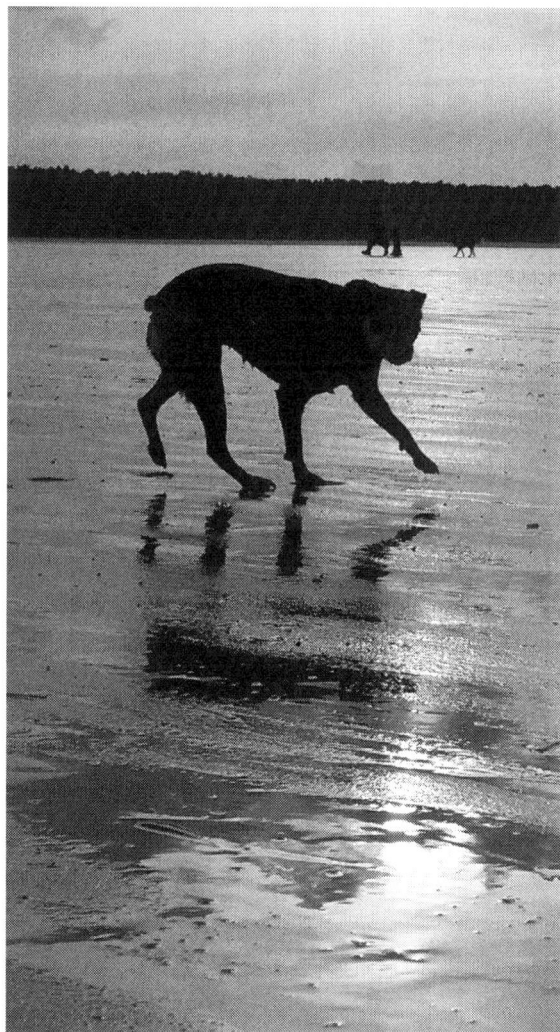

What Are these Glows we See

Bring back all the memories,
Swing on in with me,
Wrap them in a ball of twine,
And never let them leave.

Tear up all the photographs,
I shall tell you how it went,
Take a chair and pour a brew,
I'll show you what they meant.

Touch and squeeze my weathered face,
Stroke these labyrinthed, wrinkled paths,
Share then what is whispered,
And I'll answer what you ask.

I pass you on this twine of mine,
First encase some tales of ours.
Throw it to the skies above,
Let is dance upon our stars.

Then pick out any glow you wish,
Unravel every nook,
But replace each strand thereafter,
For another one to look.

We were the lost gatekeepers,
We were each other's tales,
We are involved in many,
We are these endless scales.

Wheat and Barley

This green lush,
This vibrant poison.
Digs deep within the soul,
Removes all else from reason,
Evolves to fractured tales of old.

Youths of rolling spirits entwined upon the heath.
Days of endless summers.
United by passion of blood, harmony and love.
Unrequited.
Undying,
Yet forever fading.

This curse is but to crave,
Rooted in the past,
Forever searching beyond.
These days are gone.
Could return with a single kiss,
Yet never do.

This is our England.
This is our danger land.
For scattered within its beauty are these ghosts.

Memories remain,
Forever change.
And whilst the summer passes,
It will return.
We will breathe this fresh sweet air again.

We will create memories new.
The lovers lost will forge new songs.

And though pictures die with these lips,
New tales will forge deep from within this scorched earth.

From within this this English soil,
Amid these curving hills.
The sun departs.
To rise again.
To forever share its glory.

Whispers

From the smallest grain of sand,
To the greatest bolder known to man,
Lies a great divide

With the softest, sweetest kiss,
To a heated exchange of passion,
Whispers only but one wish.

Every culture has its song,
Every meaning just as strong.
A simple tea made from me to you,
Is a happy love and a wonderful brew

I awoke for you.
I made plans simply to be beside your thoughts.
Now the wind it sings too.
Like smiles of an unstoppable force,
Like fruit cut from its hold.

How do you talk with angels,
And do you now know my voice.

With Sand Between Her Toes

I saw you one evening by the waking of the waters.

Under one arm was a basket,
Its contents I could not say,
Your feet were free of clothing,
And walked on sands that laid.

To your hair you were attending, and I watched as it you washed.

In the other hand you gathered,
An assortment of scented flowers.
Lady nature was your mistress,
For you stop snow and showers.

Rest your head on curly locks and rest equally your eyes.

Night visions you shall gather,
Like walking by the shore.
I saw the blossoms in your hair,
And I shall see this ever more.

With Passing Smiles

With the passing of loved ones, we lose not only them, but also a part of ourselves through the pain that something will forever be lost and never regained.

This unselfish selfishness is reflected in all by a recurring pattern throughout all living things.
To mourn is to remember with a smile the moments that gave to us a better, more comfortable space and upon reflection the fragility of even the strongest is realised.

Although existence is not continuous, memories and stories are,
To be passed on to loved ones for them to learn, be grateful and to admire.
If we have touched at least one in our own lifetime then a mark can be scrawled on the dusty chalkboard and with remembrance we can ensure it remains,
Amid continuous echoes to never be rubbed away.

Therefore, it is best for us to hold close to our hearts those who leave us here to carry on in their footsteps.
For whilst it is impossible to defeat the inevitable, what we do have can be cherished eternally and can be cherished by all.

Battles are never lost; rather we take our moment to depart at different stages, with or without goodbyes or the wish for those final words to have been said.
If the sun should never set on an argument then in turn it should never rise upon regret.

They are always here as we are,
And they are always there,
As we too one day will be.

Before You're Gone

As I touch you now,
Warmth exudes.
Pulse beats,
But all is cold.
Deep flickering eyes are set,
Sweet wonderful scent is stale.

And what I whisper to you now,
Are words you never shall hear.
Perfect words of devotion,
Of love,
Of bliss.

I miss these cheeks I squeeze.
Long for this head I kiss.
Exhale a breath upon me,
Though your lungs they share no air.

I may be present,
But I have never now been further.
Stood firm at different points.
And I try to be this moment,
But it has already passed.

Damn this,
Damn you,
Damn me,
Damn us.
For all this fragility.
For the fear.
For the distance in this embrace.

Nothing ever lasts forever.
Except forever.

Printed in Great Britain
by Amazon